CW00864009

The
THE PLAINS

The
THE PLAINS

MANUEL PELAEZ

Library of Congress Control Number:		2018906296
ISBN:	Hardcover	978-1-9845-3101-8
	Softcover	978-1-9845-3100-1
	eBook	978-1-9845-3099-8

To order additional copies of this book, contact:
Xlibris
1-888-795-4274
www.Xlibris.com
Orders@Xlibris.com
780155

MAIN CHARACTER

HUGH GUNPHY (RAZOR)

SON OF MAIN CHARACTER

JONATHAN GUNPHY

WIFE OF MAIN CHARACTER   SUSAN GUNPHY

FATHER OF MAIN CHARACTER   DEVIN GUNPHY

HISTORICAL EVENT

BERNARD MONTGOMERY

WORLDWIDE INTELLIGENCE AGENCIES

INTRODUCTION

To all my readers, and non readers who are drawn to the world of literature. My first goal is to bring future realities and solutions worldwide, wherever possible. Educating my fans, even though the action novel books are fictional, there's many realities within them.

My second goal is to salute my predecessors, for me they are like the special beings on earth, bringing entertainment across our globe, in all fields, books, movies, music, cinema, and many more amazing things, thanks to literature, and the fans everywhere.

PART 1

My name is Hugh, and I used to believe in love, in happiness, in a greater God, in any sort of a smile, used to wake up with hope, full of life, wishing for a better tomorrow, a future, a bright day.

My soul was broken, when my only son was viciously killed, by the hands of terrorist, blown up into pieces.

He was my only friend, the closest thing to holiness.

In one day, the school bus he was in, had a bomb, and my son, with 20 more students, were blown to kingdom come, they were headed to a field trip, (it was suppose to be a day of dinghy sailing, keel boating, catamaran sailing, team building games, paddle boarding, windsurfing, surfing, iron man style team games, kayaking, raft building, and racing).

My son Jonathan was only 12 years old, and the other students were between the ages of 12 and 14, (the perpetrators were never caught, many radical terrorist groups claimed responsibility).

The pain left me dead inside, I have no soul, my wife, his mom fell ill years afterwards, and past away, Susan was only 45 years old, she worked as a school teacher in a private elementary school for many years, deep depression, and diagnosed with a rare desease called (TTP) rare blood disorder, Thrombotic Thrombocytopenic Púrpura, blood clots form in small blood vessels in the body clots can limit or block the flow of oxygen rich blood to the major organs causing damage to the brain, heart, and kidney, also known as Moschcowitz Syndrome, symptoms include strokes, fever, hallucinations, numbness, fits, and difficulty speaking.

What a life, full of misery, suffering, absolute madness, I had to leave the city of London, in England, before I ended up insane.

I ended up coming to South Africa, and from there I joined some militants, and setting up camp, in a place called the plains.

This camp is the last stop for monsters, the worse criminals on earth, the worse of the worse.

A underground camp off the books from the world, here the secret agencies worldwide, bring me their offenders, it could be anyone.

What happens here, stays here, my nickname now is Razor, I'm 48 years old, and I specialize in curving up people slowly, and torturing them until their vocal cords give out.

My best friend is a commando knife, extremely sharp blades, here in the plains, you can hear the screams for miles, I keep a campfire on continuously, to light up a torch, I always start with the burning of feet first.

I take my time, no rush, this place is your last stop in life, I take the life out of people, piece by piece.

I truly feel like I'm doing a greater service, purifying the world of evil, I get happy when governments bring me a bus load of offenders.

Nothing here exists, to the outside world, the private landing field is close by.

My crew are all ex-military, and are completely loyal to me, my babies, a farm of 40 komodo dragons (Varanus Komodoensis), most are 3 meters (10 ft) weighing over 70 kilograms (150 lbs), venomous bite two glands in lower jaw secrete several toxic proteins, the glands have anticoagulant, capable of running rapid sprints up to 20 km/h (12 mph), diving up to 4.5 m (15 ft), they can climb trees also.

The compound is many acres, with lakes, trees, and a massive wall surrounding it, they are feed well, the remains of the offenders, and

living ones as well, using a stop watch to see how many minutes they are completely devoured.

They look like modern day dinosaurs, they don't leave nothing behind.

Agreements are made with all countries involved to assist in the transport of criminals, terrorist, habitual offenders, gang leaders, the most dangerous, they arrive secretly by military cargo plane, with military fighter jets escort, only by military plane the criminals are brought in, (even if in the same continent of Africa), once unloaded they are transported by a modified light armored passenger bus with military ground escorts, around the entire compound, scrambling towers are in place, not allowing any tracking location of the compound.

Land and air, are covered by heavily armed helicopters, armored vehicles, and soldiers carrying M249 light machine guns, 5.56 mm, 50 rpm to 100 rpm.

The compound itself is well guarded, around the clock, using advanced technologies, everyone is well trained.

The worse offenders are first, no time wasted, as much as eleven at a time, they are tied up with chains.

My crew has to wear ear plugs to block out the screams, I don't wear any ear plugs, the screams are my music.

My father Armory Sergeant Devin Gunphy, served in World War Two, in the British Army, and miraculously survived the battle of the bulge, 12-16-44 through 1-25-45, a German offensive campaign in the western front, in the densely forested Ardennes region of Wallonia in eastern Belgium, northwest France, and Luxembourg.

Field Marshal Bernard Montgomery ordered xxx corps back to the Netherlands, British and Canadian casualties were approximately 1,400 killed, wounded and missing.

It was total hell, I remember one story my father told me about, where he was among a few survivors, buried underneath many dead bodies, a fog covered the vast lands, he couldn't believe he was alive.

Waiting many hours, forgetting about time, he slowly started to walk out, he witnessed several hundreds, perhaps more, dead bodies, body parts everywhere, and somehow he had to get the will to continue.

He was a quiet man, I can only imagine everything he witnessed in his life, he died peacefully many years after the war, my moments with him will always be in a special place, and hearing those stories, gave me courage and a sense of the harsh reality of life.

My resume is impressive, but it all came to an end with unimaginable tragedies, at 18 years old, I joined the British Army, and slowly made it up the ranks.

I made it into the (SFSG) Special Forces Support Group, there I became a trained assassin, going on many assignments, and seeing the horrors of war up close, seeing what men are capable of doing to other men.

I was able to join the secret intelligence service (SIS) known as (MI6), for my service and know how of expertise in many fields, I was studying while in the special forces, to obtain my masters degree.

I made many contacts worldwide with other secret intelligence agencies, but when that event happened to my only young son, and afterwards the illness to my wife, I became a broken soul.

The secret intelligence service (MI6) offered me early retirement, with full benefits and incentive package, everyone knew my heart was hurting badly.

I tried living in London, but the memories were haunting me, so I decided to go to South Africa, there I met up with some of my brothers from the British Army, and others, that were in the special forces.

We became militants, and the idea of getting several acres of land with lake came to me, and create what is known as the plains.

By using all my money, connections, and private donations across the globe, it became a reality, with time we received military equipment from many governments, coordinate with other secret intelligence agencies everywhere.

The politics of this operation is simple, rid the world of infested regions, where cartels, gangs, criminal organizations, everyone who is evil, is sent here, off the records, off the grid, it doesn't exist, nor does the personal brought here.

By plane, 44 prisoners are brought in every month, like clock work, from many countries, I make it crystal clear, that I don't torture priests, or pastors, or individuals, that have truly repent from their sins, which isn't hard to notice, (but when one chooses to become a monster, they shall be treated like a monster).

I only want hardcore evil people, that are true to their cause, and stopped being human altogether, most are worse than animals, tattoos on their faces, bodies, some are the opposite, especially the leaders of cartels, (living in absolute luxury).

Their crimes are beyond disgusting, and they have no remorse whatsoever.

Even countries that have no human rights, once in a while when they get a high profile gang leader, which buy the neighborhoods, and are generous to the regular towns people, prefer to kidnap those individuals, and just send them here, to avoid riots in the streets, and mobilize their armies.

I remember when I worked for the secret service, a story that was told about a man falling from a tree, into a group of komodo dragons, only to be torn into pieces within minutes.

I later became obsessed with that species, and traveled to see them up close, the komodo dragon (Varanus Komodonsis), also known as komodo monitor.

This species is found in Indonesian Islands of Komodo, Rinca, Flores, Gili Motang, and Padar, being in this region I became good friends with the handlers, scientists, and experts, gathering vital intel, and connections, to build my own farm one day.

The compound itself took years in the making, myself with the right connections, put together squads of ex army commandos, ex agents, some with knowledge of building contractors, knowledge of machinery, renting bulldozers, cranes, and making the compound possible.

The komodo dragons farm has a wall surrounding the perimeter, and a manual wheel type slide with hatch to deliver the food, once anything is put on the slide, turning the wheel, the slide starts from the bottom and goes up into a slide, straight into the hatch, once the food is dropped, the hatch closes instantly.

The slide is a tunnel like chamber, with a ball type arm device in the back, which pushes the food forward, the food can be large prey, once inside the slide, the ball type arm device pushes forward it's impossible to stop, the food is carried from bottom to top, it's not that tall, around 8 feet in height.

The komodo dragons have developed a ferocious appetite for human flesh, they are extreme carnivores, and don't leave any trace of their victims.

My dream is to rid the world of the infestation of terrorist camps, gangs, cartels, and especially the financial servants, which helps make these monsters possible, causing an endless amount of suffering to innocent people in many regions.

Myself and my hand picked squads, are rewarded financially, and are souls are being cleansed, of the evil poison of this world.

Many regions across the globe have overwhelming amounts of gangs, and cartels, mostly in South America, Central America, Mexico, and terrorist occupation zones, in many Middle East countries, and elsewhere.

In Europe criminal organizations are formed, in the United States, many gangs, have taken over neighborhoods, across Asia in many regions also, it looks like a endless battle, not to mention the financial trails making them possible to operate.

Many countries see this growing problem as a present and future problem, that is depleting valuable resources by building more prisons everywhere, housing thousands of inmates, and many are running criminal activities from within the prison systems.

This problem is getting worse, building more enormous prisons, and housing thousands of inmates is not sustainable, many lifers are not given the death penalty, the inmates are getting better coordinated from inside the prisons, even running a social order.

Crime and corruption, is costing taxpayers trillions of dollars, and causing civilians to flee their countries, the gangs, and cartels, are infesting neighbors everywhere, furthermore, the terrorist are taking advantage of the breakdowns in law enforcement agencies.

There is no easy answers, but at least I'm bringing solutions, to an endless problem, it might seem barbaric, but try to hear the stories of suffering from so many innocent civilians.

Rouge governments are creating terrorist training camps, cartels are manufacturing drugs in many countries, causing murder rates to climb off the charts, and poisoning other nations, gangs are rising out of control, causing civilians to become refugees, by abandoning their

countries of origin, bank corruption is causing interest rates to climb, making things unbearable for normal working people.

The compound is a underground solution, to many unwanted answers, a necessity to a worldwide epidemic, that is growing out of control, and causing corruption, even within government employees, law enforcement, city officials, leaving a dark financial blueprint in it's path.

The entire compound operation is completely off the grid, not on any records, no paper trail, not even the United Nations knows about this operation.

Since it's located in another country, there is no human rights, no laws, since it doesn't exist, no one to answer to.

It's been already three years that this compound has been opened, and I recall some of my memorable moments, going back since the beginning.

At first, countries were figuring out, how to coordinate the inmates, since many regions were involved, only the worst criminals were chosen, some were completely different.

For example, out of forty four men, and sometimes very rare some women, the worse gang members, have tattoos even on their faces, I don't care what's the name of their gangs, or how powerful they are, some of them are cartels, which are extremely dangerous also, the leaders have lived a lifestyle of the rich and famous, I don't care what region they are from, some are just brutal murderers, assassins, hit men, some are bankers, in the black markets, money laundering, etc.

In many rare occasions, high profile criminal leaders, anything from gangs, to distribution of drugs, massive farms with many acres, housing laboratories.

Some communist countries, even though they execute a lot of criminals, the ones that have helped out regular citizens in small towns and

neighborhoods, those countries prefer to vanish them, and bring them here, to avoid riots, from erupting in their cities.

Other countries, have terrorist breeding camps, operating in secret locations, right under their noses, those countries, also prefer to vanish those individuals, because they can easily grow in numbers, and overrun their own governments, and takeover their countries.

However you put it, the justice for many types of hardcore criminals which have no remorse, no redemption, and have brought endless amounts of suffering to so many innocent people, these criminals are beyond the standards of humanity.

I know we don't live in a perfect world, but this compound is cleansing one region at a time, one country at a time, one city at a time, one neighborhood at a time, one town at a time, one village at a time.

It's not an easy solution, but until other solutions that make sense comes fourth, the compound will continue in operation.

PART 2

When the first plane arrived, all forty four criminals were in chains from neck to legs, (but still able to walk very slowly), an arrangement has been made that all criminals must be wearing shorts only, for obvious reasons, when tortured it's easier, and when dropped into the komodo dragons farm.

The criminals all slowly walk towards their cells, they stay in chains the entire time, they all taught that this compound is another prison, where they can serve out their life sentences, if they only knew, that here, eleven criminals see death in just three days, every three days out of the week they parish, two days of every week myself and the squads rest up, depending on clean up and other matters, (like wash downs of cells, the criminals are treated like farm animals).

Eleven criminals are taken out in chains, wearing only shorts, and all eleven are wearing dust masks, which we keep boxes in stock, to prevent them from spitting on me, and to allow them to scream as much as possible.

Ten steel poles are placed next to each other, only five feet apart, with steel chains to secure each criminal, one steel pole is placed directly in front of the ten steel poles, this is reserved for the strongest will, that cannot be broken, all the steel poles are in a concrete based foundation.

If for any reason any criminal is able to make a run to nowhere, there's a sniper on top to take them out instantly with a head shot.

I recall more then once, when all eleven criminals are secured on the poles, the one directly in front of the ten poles, started laughing nonstop, at first I taught he was crazy, but then realized he just doesn't care.

When that happened, I turned my attention to that individual, and the way I usually start off, on the ground there's a campfire on, the reason for this, is to lite up a torch which is always next to the campfire.

Believe me, when I start burning his feet, even the toughest criminals start to yell, they try to hold the pain, but it's way to much, after they yell for sometime, I proceed to the other criminals, hearing all of them yelling at different points, and then I usually follow up with slicing them, in different places, pouring alcohol on the wounds, and salt.

Even the toughest men cry, they yell so much, that it can be heard miles away, I have tested it, when their vocal cords can't yell anymore, which doesn't take long, hours and hours of screaming at their peaks, will do that.

Then they are ready for the slide, unable to walk, they are put in back of a flatbed truck, only a few at a time and chained, once they are placed on the slide, they are extremely weak and hardly mobile, (the restraints are reduced), where their bodies are lifted, and put into a tunnel like slide, then dropped into the farm of komodo dragons, they are ripped to pieces in just minutes, the wall has some parts in reinforced glass to see the spectacle.

Witnessing this event is beyond anything anyone can imagine, the komodo dragons are always starving, they tear entire pieces of flesh, and devour anything that drops into the slide, they have developed a special scent, and flavor for human flesh.

I specialize in taking the beast out of anyone, and have no pity for these monsters that have caused so much suffering.

I recall the times where cartel members offering to give vital information before meeting their fate, those individuals I record what they say, it's worth a lot to many governments, and in exchange something is always

worked out, but most of the time, the cartels go out in a nightmare type fashion, as do everyone here.

On occasions the corrupted bankers, which are just as guilty, many of them offer hidden amounts of cash, thinking that they can buy themselves out of situations, those individuals I gather their information, like routing and account numbers, and locations, but they still meet their fate.

Corruption doesn't exist here, because I truly believe in what this compound is about, and making the world better, even though I acknowledge there are corrupt governments, and evil nations, that have great armies protecting them, but that's another issue altogether.

My special criminals, are terrorist, that believe deep in a cause, which don't hesitate to cause massive amounts of damage, weather it's blowing themselves up among innocent bystanders, or can place bombs just about anywhere, killing whoever, wherever, at any location, they do not discriminate, any age, any gender, any race.

The goal, the use of violent tactics such as bombings and assassinations for achieving perceived Islamic goals.

Definition of extremism, vocal or active opposition to western fundamental values, including democracy, the rule of law, individual liberties, and mutual respect and tolerance of different faiths and beliefs, related terms include, the ideology of Islamism (political Islam) radical Islam and Islamic supremacy.

Terrorist are worst then the cartels and gangs, because they don't do it for money, drugs, turf, or corruption, they truly believe deeply and spiritually in their cause.

The absolute destruction of western civilizations, going back to ancient times, and the Prophet Muhammad, even though the Quran is suppose to be peaceful, understanding the Muslims history is important.

The four holy books in Islam, Zabur is, according to Islam, the holy book of Dawud (David), one of the holy books revealed by God before the Quran, alongside others such as the Tawrat (Torah) of Musa (Moses) and the Injil (Gospel) of Isa (Jesus).

Some scholars equate the Zabur with the biblical book of Psalms.

The Quran is the holy book for Muslims, revealed in stages to the Prophet Muhammad over 23 years.

Quranic revelations are regarded by Muslims as the sacred word of God.

Intended to correct any errors in previous holy books such as the old and new testaments.

Muslims believe that the Quran was verbally revealed by God to Muhammad through the angel Gabriel (Jibril), gradually over a period of approximately 23 years, beginning on 22 December 609 CE, when Muhammad was 40, and concluding in 632, the year of his death.

I recall in the beginning when the compound was in operation, a plane loaded with 44 terrorist arriving, a tight group, here no special accommodations, no special requests, no human rights whatsoever.

When eleven were secured with chains, and onto the steel poles, they all were yelling something in another language, like some type of a spiritual event, but when I started with the torch, the burning of the feet, it slowly turned into high peak screaming, listening to the group screaming at the sky, waiting to see anything.

Hours and hours pass by, being sliced open in many parts, with wounds everywhere, when I pour alcohol and salt on the wounds, even more screaming comes out, only until the vocal cords can't anymore, they're on their way to the slide.

Remember, there are snipers above if by any miracle, which is almost impossible, because how weak they are, to be mounted on the slide, if one decides to run to nowhere, the sniper takes them out instantly with a head shot.

Ever since the compound has been in operation, criminals everywhere are trying not to get caught, or vanish, the terrorist camps are more secretive, further into vast lands, and trying to become smarter, but it's always an endless supply.

Criminals, gangs, bank corruption, terrorist, will always exist, and the compound is a difficult solution, to an overwhelming problem.

My only regret is knowing that some governments are beyond evil, but they run massive countries, that have powerful armed forces, to protect them constantly, they are just as guilty.

Trying to bring the leaders and their generals, to any justice is almost impossible, they have advanced technologies, the latest weaponry, even nuclear weapons.

My conscious is in the right place, in a imperfect world, surrounded by so many complicated issues, and political views, many interests worldwide.

I know I'm making some difference, even though it takes time, but at least the monsters that society is afraid of, end up here, where they take their last breath.

My spirit is at peace, knowing that these monsters will not spend years and years depleting resources, costing taxpayers trillions of dollars, in operating their criminal empires in many cases from inside the prison walls.

The answer lies perhaps somewhere in the middle, because building endless massive facilities, with arces and arces of land, spending

hundreds of millions of dollars on each prison, even more for super max security prisons, isn't the answer either.

I'm still waiting for the day to see anything formed in the skies above, any unusual signs, to retire from this damnation, and be healed everywhere, when and if that ever happens, someone else will take my place, (it's extremely hard to juggle evil and good).

What in the world, can I say to God, whenever I decide to be set free of my internal burning, will he ever forgive me for acting out, or will he embrace me, one thing is for sure, sometimes, I feel my spirit calling out to him.

Remember, I was a normal happy individual, with a loving family, surrounded by joy and happiness, until one day, everything in stages came crashing down on me, unable to think, I tried to work, I tried everything, but the pain, the memories, consumed me.

I know that their are many out there, that have suffered so much, but those individuals can rest assured, that these monsters sooner or later, end up here, and I promise, they will be screaming for hours and hours, up to the sky, until they can't anymore.

Then my babies can tear them from limb to limb, only taking breaks to breathe.

These modern day dinosaurs, are eating machines, they are so fierce, that even I don't dare to have any contact with them, over the years they have acquired a ferocious appetite for human flesh.

Who knows what the future will bring, perhaps more compounds, maybe worse, I've heard stories of black market harvesting vital organs, and whatever is needed in the underground markets, some countries practice barbaric practices, and see inmates that have life sentences, a waste of time, they are treated like animals.

Who knows what's going on in reality in secret, but some problems are extremely complicated, and require all sides to be heard, collecting point of views, analyzing data, financial costs, getting everyone involved, to compromise, and find results to this crisis.

Five hundred twenty eight criminals come each year to the compound, it may not seem like much, but remember most countries have the death penalty, even though it takes years, others have executions, other alternatives are Guantanamo base detention camp, or super max prisons, which costs taxpayers, and the criminals are there for years.

Who knows what the future holds, either more compounds, or other solutions, one thing is for sure, there is no easy answers, to some what impossible questions, or outcomes, every taxpayer, every citizen, every voter, in every country, city, neighborhood, town, village, must decide what is best.

CPSIA information can be obtained
at www.ICGtesting.com
Printed in the USA
BVHW03*1007290618
520434BV00004B/20/P

9 781984 531018